D0922404

Cat and Mouse get a pet

Ray Gibson

Reading consultant: Karen Bryant-Mole

Designed and illustrated
by Graham Round

Edited by Paula Borton

Parent's notes

This book is for you and your child to use together. It is aimed at children aged three and up who are just ready to learn to read their first words. It contains early reading activities which will help bridge the gap between prereading activities and first solo storybooks.

The main purpose of the book is to build your child's confidence and give a positive attitude to reading. It does not follow one particular method of teaching reading, but takes a varied approach which will not conflict with anything your child is learning at school.

On some pages there is just a simple story for you to read to your child. Being read to is a very important part of the process of learning to read. Feeling that books are a source of pleasure provides children with a strong incentive to read by themselves. It also helps to improve their listening and concentration skills and to develop their sense of what a story is.

There are instructions on each page to tell you what to do and footnotes to explain how the activity is contributing to your child's reading skills. The words in blue are for your child to read. Point them out and help your child to guess what they say.

The book builds towards a simple story for your child to read alone. The words used in the story are all introduced and used earlier in the book.

When tackling any of the activities in this book, go at your child's natural pace and give plenty of praise and encouragement. It is very important that your reading sessions are enjoyable.

How do you know if your child is ready to read?

There is no definite way of knowing the answer to this. There are, however, some questions you could ask yourself to help you decide.

- Does your child like books?
- Does your child sometimes look at them alone?
- Does your child sometimes pretend she is reading?
- Does your child show an interest when you point out words, or write things down?
- Can your child recognize her own name?

- Does your child know a few letter sounds?
- Does your child ask you what words say?
- Does your child sometimes join in when you read stories she knows well?
- Can your child retell a simple story in the right sequence?

If your answer to most of these questions is "yes", then your child is probably ready to read.

Meet Cat and Mouse

This is Cat.   This is Mouse.   They live together in this house.

Who likes cooking?   Who likes cars?   Who likes looking at the stars?

Who likes puzzles?   Who builds bricks?   Who likes doing magic tricks?

Cat's clearing all their things away.   They're going to choose a pet today.

Choosing a pet

Cat and Mouse are very excited. Today, they are going to the pet shop to choose a pet to come and live with them. The trouble is they can't decide which pet to have.

They look in a book about pets which Mouse found in the library.

Cat likes the hamsters, but Mouse likes the rabbits. Cat likes the fish, but Mouse likes the parrots. Cat likes the snakes, but Mouse likes the spiders. They just cannot agree.

"There's only one way to decide," says Mouse. "We must go and look in the shop and then make up our minds."
"I agree," says Cat.
"That's the first time we've agreed today," says Mouse.

hamster   rabbit   parrot   fish

Which house?

"If we choose a pet," says Mouse, "we'll have to find a house for it."
Can you see which pet belongs in which house?

fish

snake

parrot

spider

hamster

Spotting pairs of matching shapes helps children recognize word shapes when they start to read by themselves.

5

What am I?

On the way to the pet shop, Cat and Mouse buy some popcorn to share.
Then they play a guessing game as they walk along.
One has to pretend to be an animal, while the other has to guess the name of it.

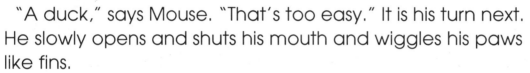

It is Cat's turn first. He flaps his arms like wings and shouts, "Quack, quack."

"A duck," says Mouse. "That's too easy." It is his turn next. He slowly opens and shuts his mouth and wiggles his paws like fins.

"A fish," says Cat. "Now it's my turn again." He stuffs both cheeks with popcorn to make them as fat as he possibly can. He twitches his nose. "What am I?" he mumbles.

"You are pretending to be a hamster, but I think you're just a greedy cat," laughs Mouse.

Pet shop

Snips

Baker

snacks

fruit

cheese

When they reach the shops, Cat and Mouse play another game.
"I spy with my little eye something beginning with 'buh'," says Mouse.
Cat guesses it is 'buh' for bread. He is right. Now it is Mouse's turn to guess.
You can pretend to be Cat and Mouse, and play the "I spy" game as
you look at the picture.

In the pet shop

At last, Cat and Mouse arrive at the shop. Inside, there are so many pets that they don't know which one to look at first. It is very noisy. Hamsters are squeaking, birds are chattering, puppies are barking, and a parrot is cackling. "I hope our pet won't make too much noise," says Cat.

"Yes. My ears are hurting," says Mouse.

"Look!" cries Mouse, "that goat has a lovely shiny coat."
"Goat and coat, that makes a rhyme," says Cat. "Let's think of other words that can rhyme with names of pets."

You can play a rhyming game too. Look at the pictures on the bottom of the opposite page and see if you can find a pet's name to rhyme with them. Can you also find six spiders hiding somewhere in the picture?

dog dog d

guinea pigs

carrot

log

wizard

coat

pen

nail

rake

Which pet?

These pictures tell the story of how Cat and Mouse decide which pet to have.

The purpose of this picture story is to encourage children to focus on what is happening in each picture and to translate this into words which build into a story.

dog 5

dog 6

parrot 7

8

Who got wet? Was it Mouse or Cat?

What noise do snakes make? Which pet would you have chosen?

Can you think of a name for Cat and Mouse's parrot?

This skill will be useful when your child comes to read stories with words. Clues from the pictures give children the confidence to try the words in the stories.

11

Parrot trouble

Read this story with your child, following the lines with your finger. When you get to the words in the blue type, stop and help your child to read them.

Cat and Mouse are very pleased to have a new pet at last. Mouse hops, skips and jumps on the way home. Cat carries the parrot in her cage. "I'm not bumping the cage too much, am I?" Cat asks the parrot.

"No," says the parrot.

" You won't mind living in our kitchen, will you?" asks Mouse.

"No," says the parrot.

"You won't eat too much, will you?" asks Cat.

"No," says the parrot.

"She's so polite, Cat," says Mouse. "I think we have chosen the perfect pet."

Mrs. Frog comes down the street. She is wearing a new hat, and looks very pleased with herself.

"How do you like my new hat?" she asks. "Do you think it suits me, Cat?" Cat opens his mouth to say something nice.

"No," says the parrot.

Mrs. Frog thinks it was Cat who spoke.

"How rude," she says and marches off. Cat does not know what to say.

Your child will soon begin to recognize the repeating words and will have a sense of achievement from helping you read the story.

"You look upset, Cat," says the baker. He is loading up his van with warm, fresh rolls. "Have one of these to cheer you up. They smell delicious, don't they?" Cat opens his mouth to say that they do.

"No," says the parrot.

The baker thinks Cat has said this.
"How rude," he says. He slams the door and drives away with all the rolls. Cat would have liked a roll to eat. He looks crossly at the parrot.
"You're getting me into trouble," he says. "Can't you be quiet, please?"

"No," says the parrot. "No, no, no."

"Don't you know any other words?" asks Mouse.

"No, no, no, no, no, no, no," says the parrot.

Cat and Mouse look at each other.
"Do you think we have chosen the right pet?" asks Mouse.

"No," says the parrot.

"I thought you'd say that," says Cat.

The chase

Read this story with your child, pausing when you come to a picture. Let your child say the word for the picture and then continue reading. Follow the lines with your finger as you read them.

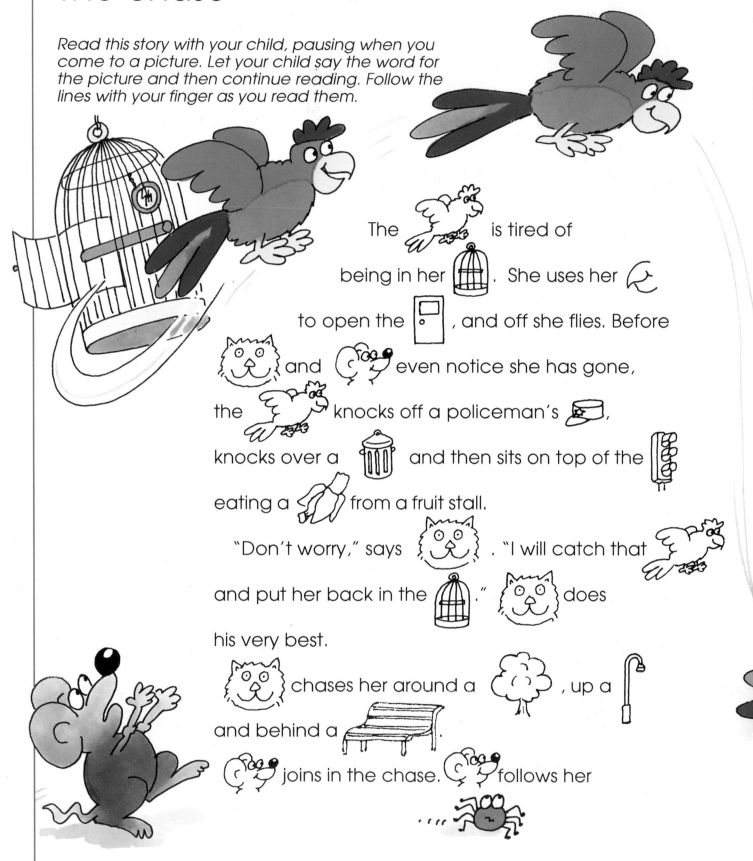

The 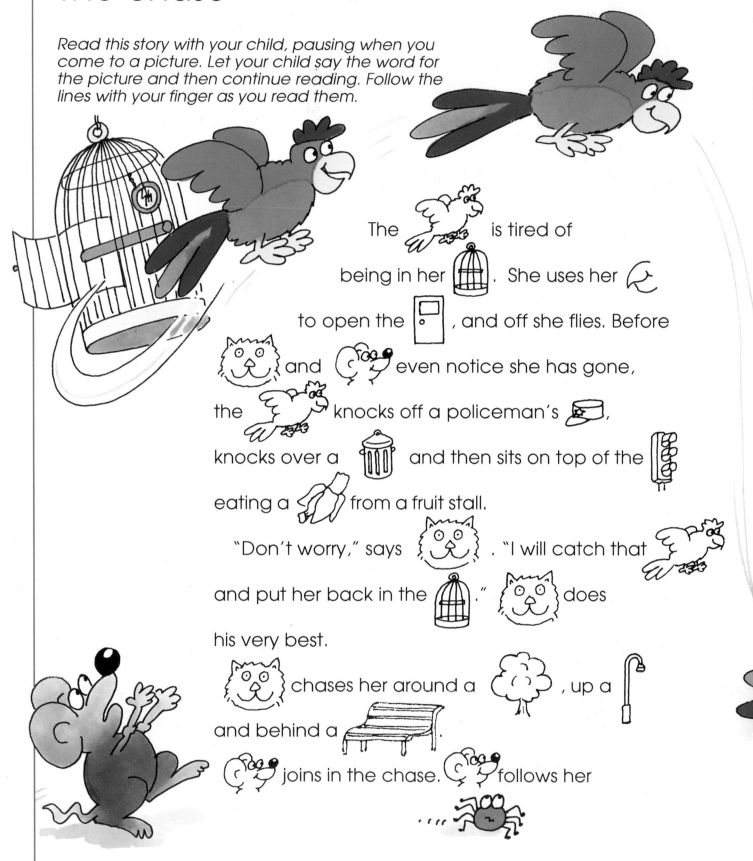 is tired of

being in her 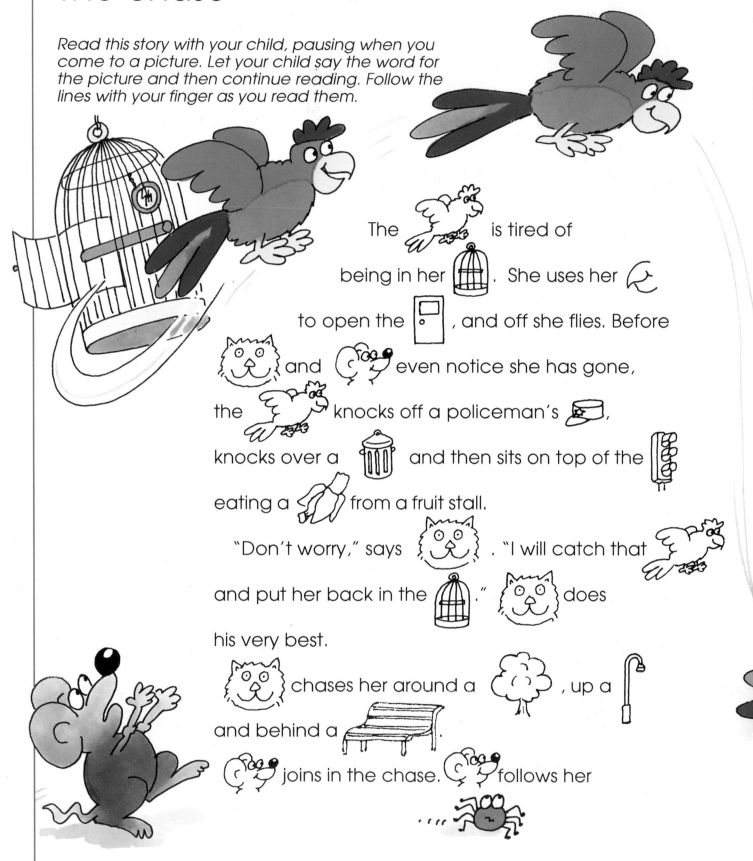. She uses her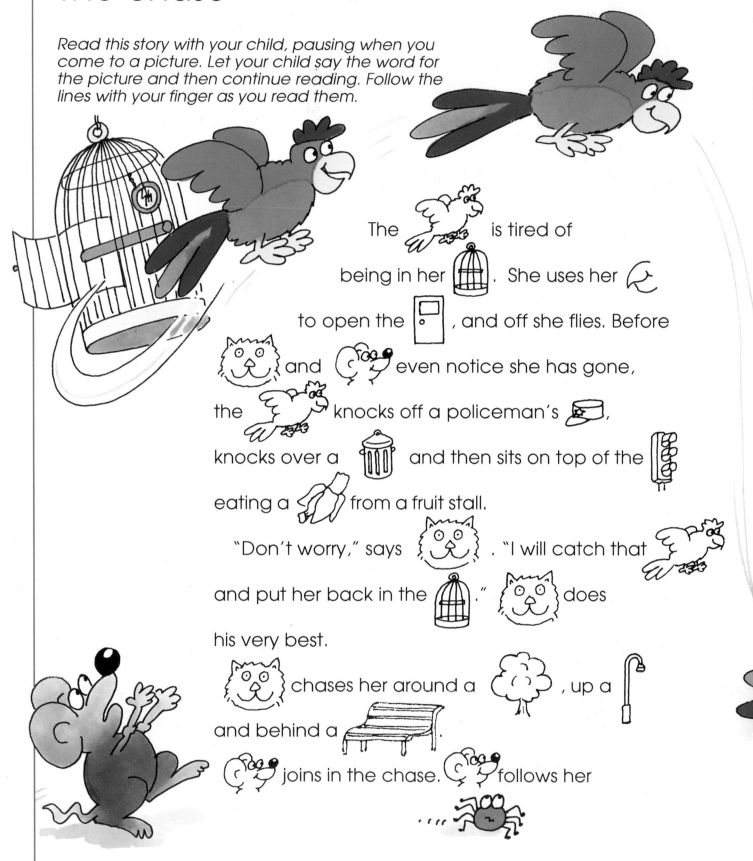

to open the 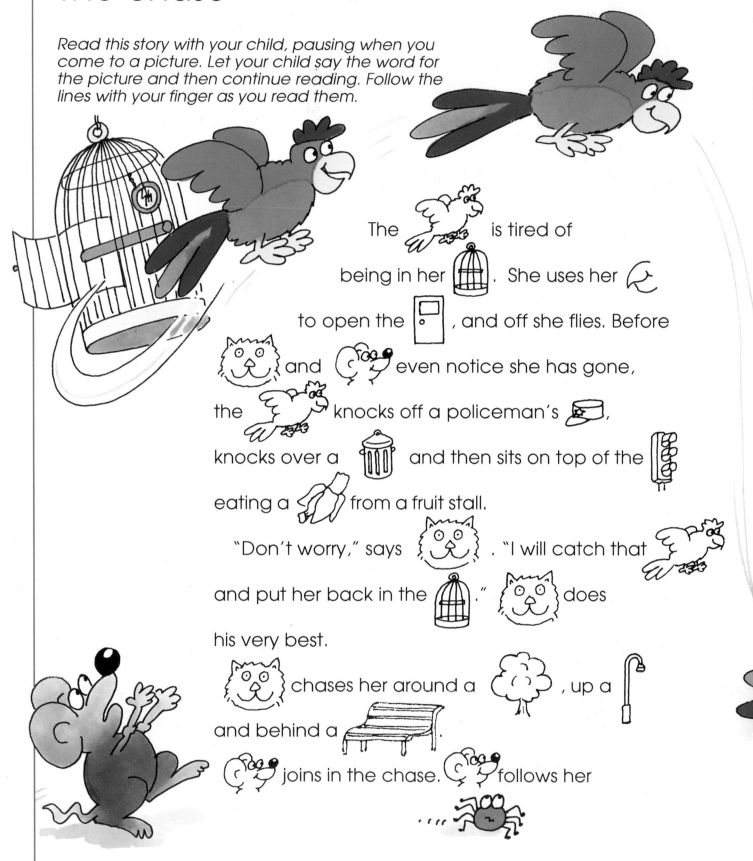, and off she flies. Before

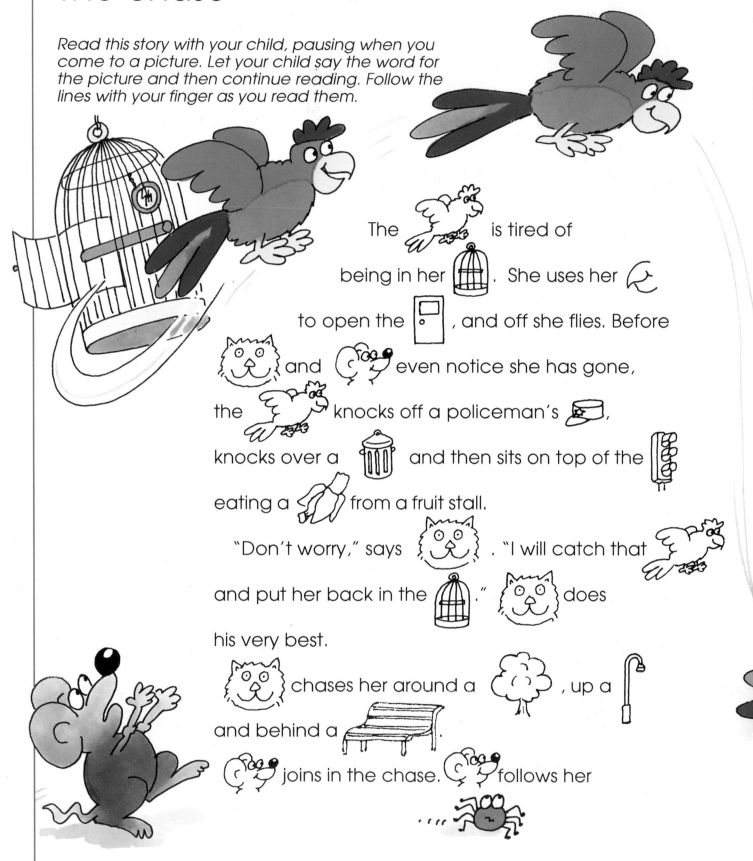 and 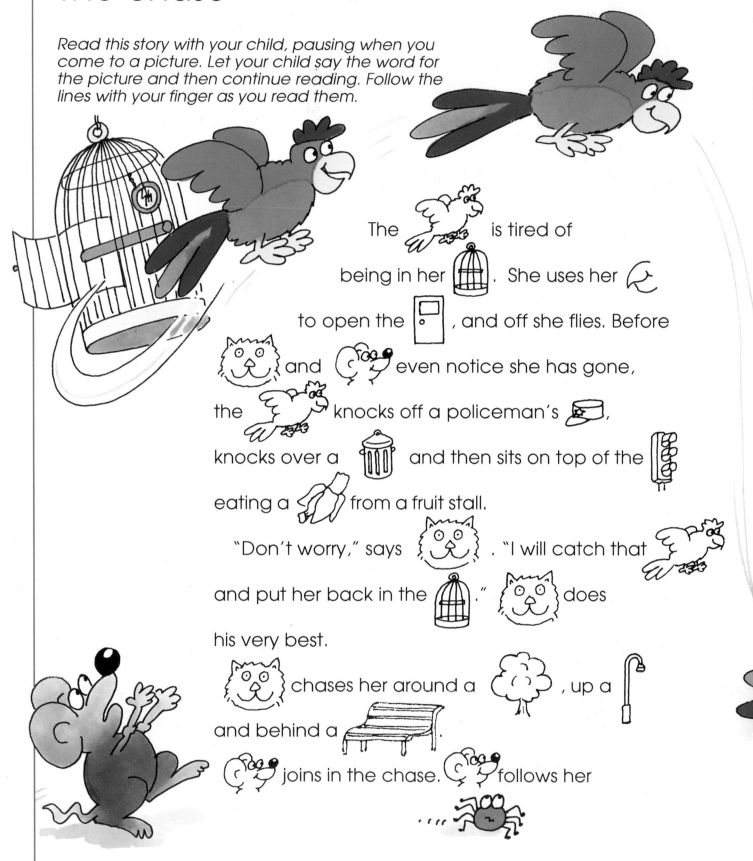 even notice she has gone,

the knocks off a policeman's ,

knocks over a and then sits on top of the

eating a from a fruit stall.

"Don't worry," says . "I will catch that

and put her back in the ." does

his very best.

 chases her around a , up a

and behind a .

 joins in the chase. follows her

under a  , over a [brick wall] and down some [stairs] .

All the time, the [parrot] screeches and squawks, and flaps her [wings].

At last, she settles on top of a tall [ladder] , and will not come down.

"I will get her down. That's my [ladder] ," says a [firefighter] . He grabs at the parrot's [tail] , but all he catches is a [feather] .

"At least we've got a part of our pet back," says [cat] .

Up and down

Cat and Mouse are still trying to catch their parrot. Follow their adventures by playing this game.

To play this game both players need five counters each, or you could cut paper squares, say five red and five blue. Then cut 12 pieces of thin, white cardboard about 4cm by 3cm (2in by 1½in) and write "up" on four and "down" on four. Draw a feather on the four leftover cards. The game is played on this double page.
   Put the cards in a paper bag and give it a good shake. One of you takes a card,

While having fun playing this word matching game, your child will start to recognize the words "up" and "down".

up

down

up

down

reads it and tries to match the word on the card to the same word on the page. So, if you pick an "up" card or a "down" card you look for the same word on the page and then cover it with one of your counters. If a "feather" card is pulled out, it means you miss a turn. Take turns picking the cards. Put the card back in the bag after each turn. If you pick a card that says "down" and there are no "down" pictures left, you miss a turn. Whoever uses up her counters first is the winner.

The blue balloon

The words on this page are for you to read to your child. The words on the opposite page are for your child. Start by reading the paragraph below. Then encourage your child to try the words under the picture opposite. Take turns to complete the story.

Cat spies the parrot on top of a wall. "Now we've got you," he cries. "You have been more trouble than twenty monkeys in a cake shop and have made more mess than a herd of elephants in a library. Come here at once."

   "No," says the parrot, and she flies off the wall. She doesn't see the blue balloon sailing by and its long string gets tangled in her claws.

   Up goes the parrot as the wind tugs the balloon higher and higher. Cat wants to catch his pet. Quickly he grabs hold of the parrot's tail and up goes Cat too.

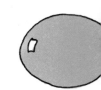

Mouse catches Cat's tail and shuts his eyes tightly. Soon, all three are floating above the trees in the park.

   "Oooooooh," wails Mouse, who doesn't like being so high.
   "Owwwww," yells Cat, who doesn't like his tail being pulled.
   "Squaaaaaawk," says the parrot, who is feeling very angry.

   A pigeon flies past. He thinks the balloon is something good to eat. He pecks it. Bang! The balloon pops, and they all fall down, down, down and land in a bush.

   "Got her, got her," cries Cat, holding on tightly. But all he has in his paws is a long piece of string, with a few raggedy bits of blue balloon on the end.

The parrot goes up.

The parrot goes up. Cat goes up.

The parrot goes up. Cat goes up. Mouse goes up.

The parrot goes down. Cat goes down. Mouse goes down.

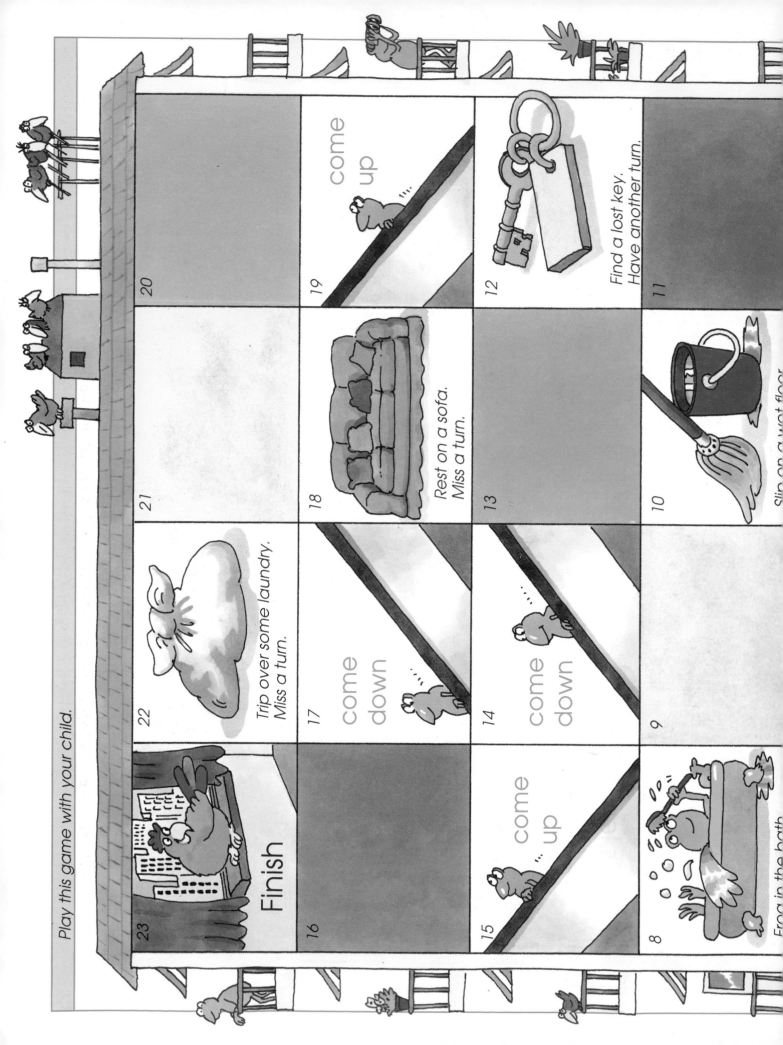

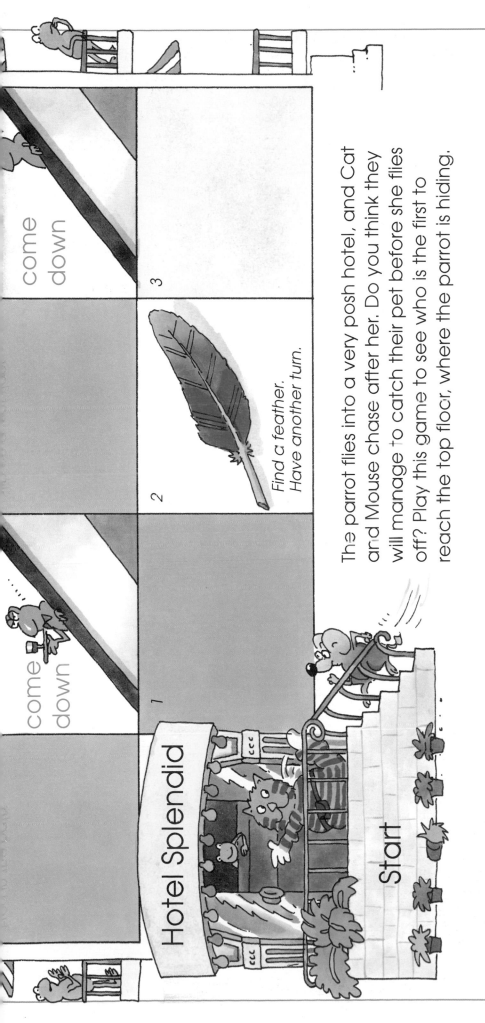

come down

come down

3

2

Find a feather.
Have another turn.

Hotel Splendid

Start

The parrot flies into a very posh hotel, and Cat and Mouse chase after her. Do you think they will manage to catch their pet before she flies off? Play this game to see who is the first to reach the top floor, where the parrot is hiding.

Playing the game

One of you can be Cat and the other is Mouse. Each of you has a counter. Put the counters on the place marked "Start". Take turns to roll a dice and move your counter along the number of squares shown by the dice. Some of the squares have instructions on them for you to follow. When you land on a square which says "come up" you can go to the square immediately above. If it says "come down" you go to the square immediately below. The winner is the first to reach room 23 where the parrot is hiding. You must roll an exact number to finish the game.

Caught

The parrot goes up.

"Come down," says Cat.

"No, no," says the parrot.

"Come down," says Mouse.

"No, no, no," says the parrot.

Cat goes up.

Mouse goes up.

Down goes the parrot.

All the words in this story have been introduced earlier in this book. Repeat some of the earlier stages if you feel your child is not ready for this yet.

23

Home at last

At last, Cat and Mouse arrive home with their new pet. They will make sure that all the windows and doors are shut before the parrot is allowed out of the cage to fly about the house.

"We haven't thought of a name for her yet," says Cat. "We must choose a name that suits her."

"I have one," says Mouse. "I think her name is Trouble. Have another piece of apple, Trouble."